FOR MISHA AND KIYO,
THE AARDVARKS WHO INSPIRED THIS STORY.

Published by
PEACHTREE PUBLISHING COMPANY INC.
1700 Chattahoochee Avenue
Atlanta, Georgia 30318-2112
www.peachtree-online.com

Text and illustrations © 2019 by Morag Hood

First published in Great Britain in 2019 by Two Hoots, an imprint of Pan Macmillan
First United States edition published in 2019 by Peachtree Publishing Company Inc.

The illustrations were created in gouache and digitally colored.

Printed in January 2019 by Leo Paper in China
10 9 8 7 6 5 4 3 2 1
First Edition
ISBN: 978-1-68263-121-8

Library of Congress Cataloging-in-Publication Data

Names: Hood, Morag (Illustrator), author, illustrator.
Title: Aalfred and Aalbert / written and illustrated by Morag Hood.
Description: First edition. | Atlanta : Peachtree Publishing Company Inc., 2019. | Summary:
Two aardvarks who lead solitary lives, Aalbert by day and Aalfred by night, sometimes
wonder if they would like to be part of a pair but how will they meet?
Identifiers: LCCN 2018052671 | ISBN 9781682631218
Subjects: | CYAC: Aardvark—Fiction. | Friendship—Fiction. | Humorous stories.
Classification: LCC PZ7.1.H655 Aal 2019 | DDC [E]—dc23 LC record available at
https://lccn.loc.gov/2018052671

AALFRED AND AALBERT

MORAG HOOD

PEACHTREE
ATLANTA

This is the story of two aardvarks.

Aalfred loved stars, broccoli, and picnics.

Aalbert loved flowers, sunshine, and cheese.

And they both loved sleeping
quite a bit, except. . .

Aalbert slept all night,

and Aalfred slept all day.

Which meant they had
never met each other.

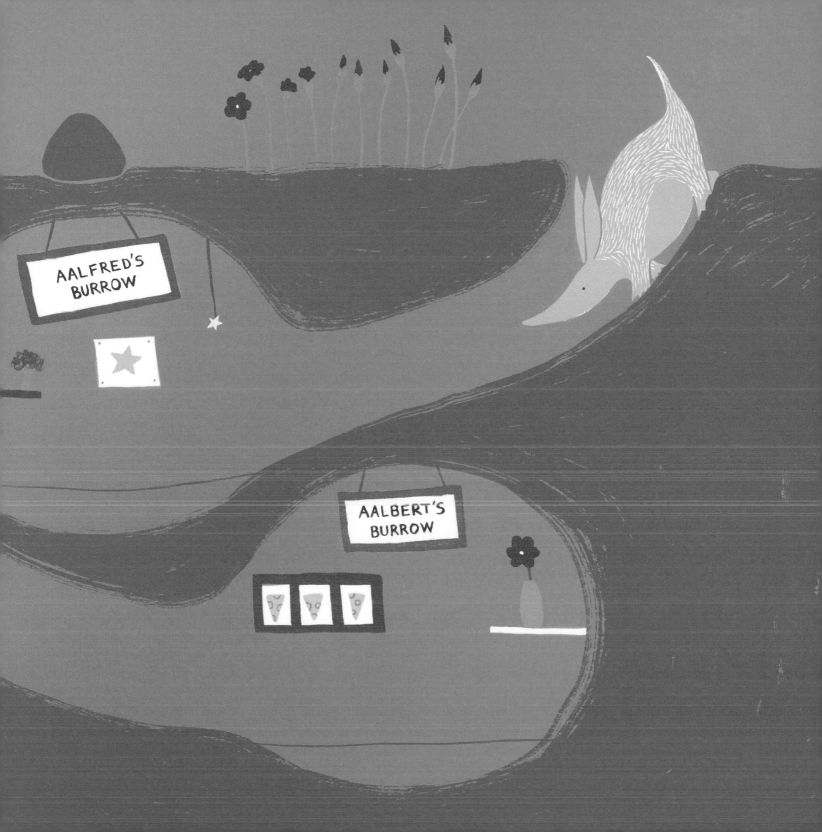

And Aalbert thought,

I might like to be one of two.

But most of the time their minds
were on other things.

Unless . . .

... somebody came up with a plan.

But nothing changed when Aalbert was woken up one night.

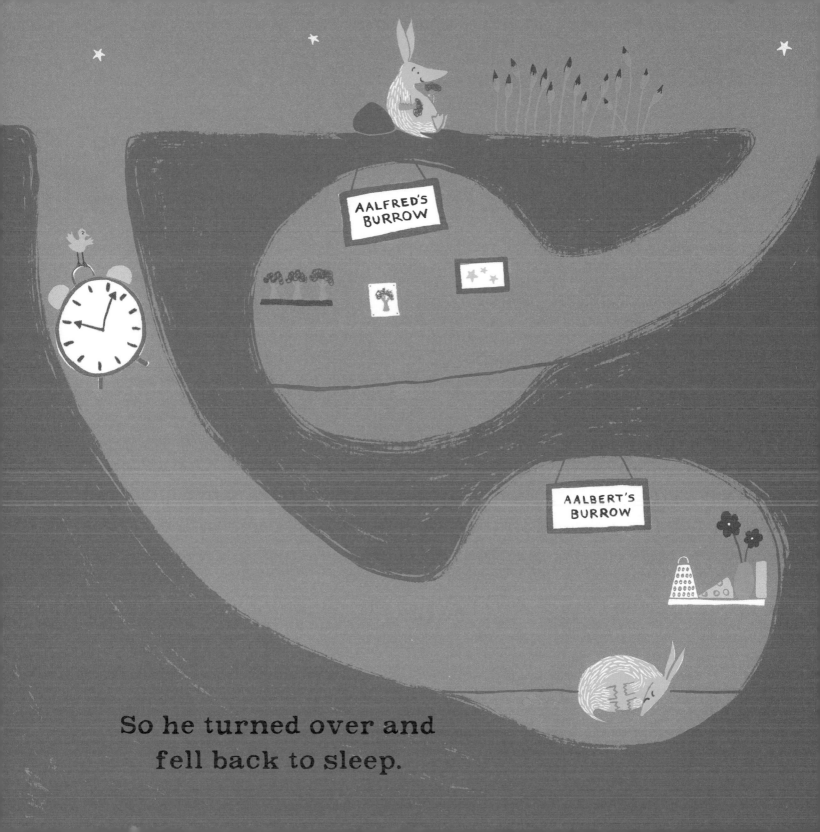

So he turned over and
fell back to sleep.

And nothing changed when Aalfred
saw something very unusual.

I wonder where that broccoli is going.

So he carried on
with his evening.

No, nothing changed. Not even when
they both got into a bit of a tangle.

It seemed nothing could bring
Aalfred and Aalbert together.

Nothing at all.

And that was very sad.

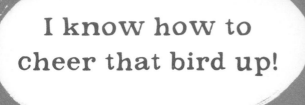

thought Aalfred.

And,

in a way,

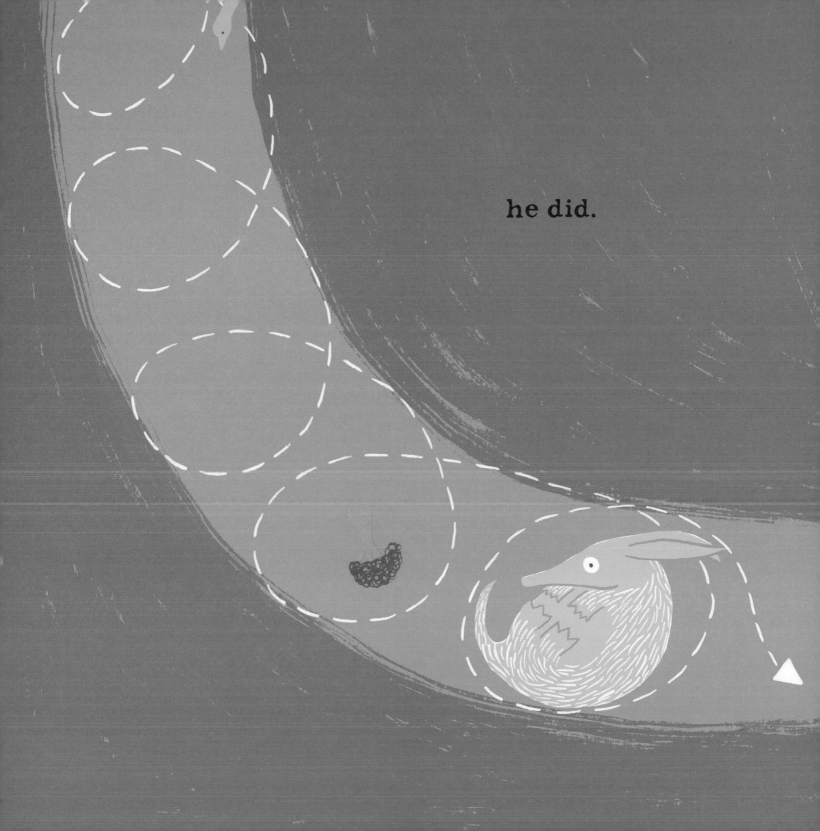

he did.

Because that is the story of
how Aalfred met Aalbert.

And they all lived happily ever aafter.